ARTHUR

Based on *The Railway Series* by the Rev. W. Awdry

Illustrations by
Robin Davies

EGMONT

EGMONT

We bring stories to life

First published in Great Britain in 2006
by Egmont UK Limited
239 Kensington High Street, London W8 6SA
This edition published in 2008
All Rights Reserved

HiT entertainment

ISBN 978 1 4052 3488 7
1 3 5 7 9 10 8 6 4 2
Printed in Italy

The Forest Stewardship Council (FSC) is an international, non-governmental organisation dedicated to promoting responsible management of the world's forests. FSC operates a system of forest certification and product labelling that allows consumers to identify wood and wood-based products from well managed forests.

For more information about Egmont's paper buying policy please visit www.egmont.co.uk/ethicalpublishing

For more information about the FSC please visit their website at www.fsc.uk.org

TO THE TRAINS →

This is a story about Arthur, a proud tank engine. He arrived on the Island of Sodor with a spotless record, but soon found himself in a sticky situation . . .

Arthur the big tank engine had just arrived on the Island of Sodor.

It was his first day at work on The Fat Controller's Railway.

"I must be on time, I must be on time," Arthur worried, as he chuffed through the countryside.

He didn't want to be late.

"Right on time!" smiled The Fat Controller. "This is Arthur. He will help you shunt trucks and pull freight."

"Nice to meet you," said Arthur, politely.

"And he's got a spotless record," The Fat Controller added.

"What's a spotless record?" whispered Percy.

"It means he's never done anything naughty," Thomas frowned.

At Brendam Docks, the three engines were soon working together. Thomas and Percy knew that they weren't supposed to bump the trucks, but it was such fun.

"Join in, Arthur!" laughed Thomas.

"No, thank you," said Arthur, quietly.

He didn't want to spoil his spotless record.

Arthur's first job was to push a line of trucks to the Market. He coupled up behind the trucks, which were loaded up with crates of fruit.

The trucks, though, were not behaving themselves and sang songs to tease Arthur.

"Root, toot, tow, come on, let's go,
The fruit's going mouldy 'cause you're too slow!"

"How rude!" huffed Arthur.

The trucks' singing gave Thomas a naughty idea.

"The Fat Controller doesn't like the trucks to sing," said Thomas. "You must tell them to stop."

"Thank you, Thomas," said Arthur. "I will."

Arthur puffed steadily out of the Docks.

"The trucks will cause trouble for Arthur if they're not allowed to sing!" laughed Thomas.

Arthur was chuffing cheerfully through the countryside, when the trucks began to sing again.

"Chug, chug, chuff, you tug and puff,
But you're too slow – you've got no puff!"

"No singing," said Arthur, firmly. "It may be my first day, but I won't fall for your tricks!"

The Troublesome Trucks were cross.

"If Arthur won't let us sing . . ." one truck whispered. "We'll teach him a lesson!" chimed the others.

The Troublesome Trucks put on their brakes and made their wheels SCREECH and SQUEAK along the tracks.

Arthur struggled over bridges . . .
And huffed and puffed through tunnels.

When poor Arthur puffed to the top of Gordon's Hill, the trucks whooshed down the other side, laughing all the way.

Suddenly, Arthur's Driver spotted a red signal at the bottom of the hill. He put on the brakes . . .

But Arthur couldn't stop in time.

Fruits of all shapes and sizes from the Troublesome Trucks flew into the air . . .

And landed: SPLAT! SPLOT! SPLAT!
All over Arthur.

Arthur was terribly sad. It was his first day on The Fat Controller's Railway and his spotless record was ruined!

Soon, The Fat Controller arrived. "What has happened here?" he said, crossly.

"The trucks were singing," said Arthur. "I told them to stop but they pushed me too fast!"

"Please, Sir, it's my fault," said Thomas, sadly. He told The Fat Controller what he had done.

"Your record is still spotless, Arthur," The Fat Controller said. "Thomas, clear up this mess at once!"

Soon, Harvey arrived with the breakdown crane and lifted Arthur back on to the rails.

Thomas stayed behind to help the Workmen clear the track.

It took a very long time to clear up the sticky mess. By the time Thomas puffed slowly home, it was dark.

When Thomas arrived back at Tidmouth Sheds, Arthur's crew had cleaned the squashed fruit from his funnel. Arthur looked spotless, and sparkled from buffer to dome!

"I'm sorry I played a trick on you," said Thomas.

"That's all right," said Arthur. "Thank you for telling the truth."

"Well, *I* never had a spotless record to ruin!" smiled Thomas.

From that moment, the engines knew they would become the best of friends.

The Thomas Story Library is THE definitive collection of stories about Thomas and ALL his friends.

5 more Thomas Story Library titles will be chuffing into your local bookshop in August 2008!

Jeremy
Hector
BoCo
Billy
Whiff

And there are even more Thomas Story Library books to follow late
So go on, start your Thomas Story Library NOW!

A Fantastic Offer for Thomas the Tank Engine Fans!

In every Thomas Story Library book like this one, you will find a special token. Collect 6 Thomas tokens and we will send you a brilliant Thomas poster, and a double-sided bedroom door hanger! Simply tape a £1 coin in the space above, and fill out the form overleaf.

TO BE COMPLETED BY AN ADULT

To apply for this great offer, ask an adult to complete the coupon below and send it with a pound coin and 6 tokens, to:
THOMAS OFFERS, PO BOX 715, HORSHAM RH12 5WG

☐ Please send a Thomas poster and door hanger. I enclose 6 tokens plus a £1 coin. (Price includes P&P)

Fan's name..

Address..

....Postcode...........................

Date of birth..

Name of parent/guardian..

Signature of parent/guardian...

Please allow 28 days for delivery. Offer is only available while stocks last. We reserve the right to change the terms of this offer at any time and we offer a 14 day money back guarantee. This does not affect your statutory rights.

☐ Data Protection Act: If you do not wish to receive other similar offers from us or companies we recommend, please tick this box. Offers apply to UK only.